TIME SQUEEZE

MATTHEW DAVID

MDM Press, USA 2012

Copyright © 2012 by Matthew David

Time Squeeze

Inside photo illustration by MDM DeSigns

Illustrated by Marita McNabb

First Printing, 2012

This book is a work of fiction. Names, characters, incidents and dialogues are the products of the author's imagination and are fictitious.

Printed in the USA

MDM Press

ISBN-13: 978-0-6157356-9-6

ISBN-10: 0-615-73569-X

For my ever supportive parents.

Prologue

North America, Ontario Border, early June, 1996

"Hurry up!"

"I'm coming."

"I'll leave without you!"

"Write in your journal or something! I'm almost done!"

"Fine!" Nathan yelled. He pulled out his diary and began to write. *Nathan Rain. We found an antechamber in a tomb. Old cemetery. Unclear what is inside, but my gut tells me something important.* Nathan stood up as he examined the aging obsidian tombstones. Almost every single one had the image of an hourglass. He frowned then went back to writing. *Tombstones have images of hourglasses. Strange markings on each one. Appears to be French. It reads: Jour de la Sablier, 30 Juin 1996. Translation: Day of the Hour, June 30, 1996.*

Nathan's friend Will climbed out of the grave. Nathan noted he had his hands behind his back. "'Bout time! What were you doing down there? Taking pictures with your mind? Dancing? And what's that grin for?"

Nathan gasped as his friend quietly handed him an ornate hourglass. It had dark blue covers on the ends, covered with intricate carvings that had no definite pattern. Lightly frosted glass made the holder and gold colored sand sparkle inside. Reverently, he took the hourglass from Will and cast his gaze over the seamless glass and smooth edges.

He looked back at Will and hesitantly asked, "Where'd you find this?" Will grinned and said, "I found it in the tomb's antechamber. It is a strange room. Get your camera. Let's go back inside, it's SWEET!"

As he stepped into the antechamber, Nathan's breath was taken away. Blue stones were everywhere making up the floors and ceiling. In the middle of the chamber stood a small, simple granite pedestal where Will had removed the hourglass from. A beam of light radiated through a small hole in the ceiling toward the four sapphires on the floor. In turn, they illuminated the space with an unfriendly eerie blue glow.

"What do you think it is?" Will asked as he motioned toward the hourglass.

The light began to dim. A low growl rumbled throughout the room vibrating with a strange intensity. Nathan swallowed hard as one of the shadows in the corner began to rise, and then another. Suddenly, two glowing red eyes appeared. Nathan grabbed at Will and scrambled out the entrance.

Both Nathan and Will ran through the grass like madmen. Will turned slightly to see Nathan close behind him. He yelled with a panicked voice, "Keep running!"

From the corner of his eye, Nathan saw what was chasing him and gasped. He glanced again at the two massive roaring things behind him. They were slightly humanoid with large hands and razor-sharp spikes covering their forearms. They also had large feet with no toes. Large limbs attached to an extremely small round torso, much like a spider. A large angled head was attached on top complete with an array of shark teeth. To finish off the already horrifying picture, fluorescent lime green lines glowed on its hands, legs, and head outlining its black bony frame. Over eight feet tall and extremely muscular, it was a nightmare come alive.

"Faster!"

"I'm moving as fast as I can with this thing!" Nathan screamed back, showing him the hourglass. As he lifted it over his head, Will and the monsters froze. The hourglass floated out of his hand, shining in an azure nimbus of energy.

He stopped dead in his tracks and turned to gape at it.

Suddenly, the hourglass dropped to the ground. Nathan cautiously approached and examined everything. The grass, the monsters, and Will were frozen solid and all color faded to shades of black and white. The golden glowing sand inside the hourglass began to drain. *"I'm thinking this hourglass is connected to freezing time and guessing I have about a minute before it drains. I'll use it to my advantage!"* While everything was still frozen, he pulled the shovel out of his pack and after many attempts, managed to destroy an arm and a leg on one monster and smash the head on the other.

He noted the sand inside the hourglass was almost depleted, and it began to crackle and turn blue again. When the sand had completely drained, a blast of white light expanded from it. Will tripped, Nathan was thrown off his feet, and the monsters fell to the ground in an agonizing wail, vaporizing.

"What happened!" asked Will. Nathan stared at where the monsters had been. All of a sudden, several dozen more materialized, screaming and coming toward them from all directions. In pure desperation, Nathan lifted the hourglass again.

Blue light exploded out of it.

He cautiously opened one eye. All the monsters had disappeared and Will stood beside him shivering.

"That . . . was . . . incredible!" Will exclaimed. He danced around in pure joy at finding this "artifact".

Nathan smiled, turned, and pulled the celebrating Will along with him.

While walking back to their camp, Nathan pulled the hourglass out again to examine it. He heard a low eerie growl behind him, "That isss my property." Without warning, he felt a sharp pain at the base of his skull and he knew no more.

Chapter 1

Outskirts of Great Falls, Montana, Present day.

"Please, Nick?"

"No.

"For me?"

"No, not even for you," I growled. "I wouldn't dream of losing to my sister."

Sarah grinned at me. "And yet you still lost to me so many times . . ." she taunted.

Enough, I thought as I slashed down at her head with my broadsword. The blunted blade would have given her a good rap on the head, if she were there, that is. She had easily dodged my swift blow and smashed her blade against mine so hard that sparks splashed everywhere. She stepped inside my guard, smashed the hilt of my broadsword with a crosscut and sent it flying from my hand. In less than a second, the flat of her blade rested on my collarbone.

I whistled, greatly impressed. "You know something?"

Sarah wiped beads of sweat from her neck. "What?"

"You're not getting any stronger."

"That's it!" My sister tore off her facemask and tackled me. We both rolled down the hill, quarreling the whole time. When we finally stopped fighting, we both picked up our swords and began dusting ourselves off. Inhuman screams suddenly echoed around the two of us.

Sarah gathered up our masks, then glanced at me, and nodded. I stabbed my sword down into the ground so hard that the blade sunk to its hilt. A low hum reverberated through the entire hill, opening a small hole, which we quickly scrambled into. I just knew if we had stayed there any longer, we would have been in grave danger.

Living independent from their parents is the dream of teenagers. However, when you are living by yourself because you have no choice, it is an entirely different story. My sister and I were born on June 30, 1996, sequestered from our parents and taught to protect the hourglass (a mystical artifact said to have the power to stop, reverse, and change time). The only thing that made this difficult was the fact that we did not have it in our possession. How are you supposed to protect something you do not even know where it is?

We walked into the poorly lit subterranean cavern where we had been living for our entire lives, about the size of a small factory. Niches were cut into the rock, where there were several workbenches with partially completed projects. There was a metal wolf-like robot whose eyes were shut. Twisted bits of metal were strewn about the cavern; containers of assorted nuts and bolts were stacked against the walls. If it existed, we probably had it: anything from coffee makers to super computers. Comfort had not been the idea in mind when this was created.

"So you cut your sparring short?" A man hunched over a small workbench called out from the shadows as we drew near.

"Yes, Professor Alden." Sarah and I called out in unison. He turned and smiled at us as we came closer. We call him Professor Alden, but he prefers Professor. We don't even know his first name. Growing up, he was our only parent figure.

He had brown eyes and his thinning gray hair stood out in every direction possible, making him appears somewhat like a crazy man. His tall, thin frame made him intimidating, and we knew from the stories he shared that he had won many battles.

Both Sarah and I laughed when were told that he would be teaching us swordplay. We changed our minds about that quickly enough after seeing him demonstrate some aggressive moves.

"Good! Then you can help me with my power shield. The final test is all that is needed. Make yourself useful, would you?"

He tossed me a small circular device about three inches in diameter. I strapped it on my wrist much like putting on a watch.

"Yo, professor, you do know that this thing couldn't stop anything . . ."

Suddenly, he turned, and violently fired repeatedly at me. The device on my wrist did not expand to meet the barrage, but created a blue bubble-like shield around me, deflecting the fire.

"What was that?" I screeched in extreme surprise (an octave higher than my normal voice). Sarah and the professor cracked up, both pointing to a blue sapphire in the middle of the small metal plate. I glanced up at him. "You're obsessed with blue, aren't you?"

"Yes, Yes!" The professor shook his head so violently that his mustache bounced. "Blue is the color of the hourglass! We must have a team color, no?"

I shook my head at him. "Have you found anything useful?"

The professor's eyes immediately lit up. "I was hoping you would ask." He whirled around, grabbed a remote, and pressed a button. "This." The sight of majestic ruins appeared on a screen complete with large, glowing monsters made it look like a cheesy horror movie set. Only, it was real.

"Where is that?"

"Canada."

"I'm assuming they're looking for the hourglass?"

The professor shrugged. "Obviously."

I turned around and shook my head. "You do know that this a bit too obvious, right? I mean, isn't he intelligent enough to go to an inconspicuous place where he would not call attention to himself? Somewhere he knows that we would not attack?"

The one I am talking about is enemy number one, the original guardian of the hourglass. Wryghten is a massive thirty-foot long floating serpent, with a nasty attitude and over six hundred years of fighting experience. In days of old, guardians were assigned to protect the hourglass from mercenaries and crime lords. He was the best guardian ever, and nobody could get past him. He was practically invincible.

Over time, his thoughts turned to anger through endless nights of waiting for anything, or nothing to happen. Then one night, he became so angry and full of rage that he decided to absorb the power of the hourglass in an attempt to make himself invincible. The hourglass would only transfer its power to ones pure of heart though, so he was not able to capture all of it. When he learned this, he decided to wait for one to come and help him retrieve the power.

Now, it is a race against time itself! Wryghten was doing his best to find anyone who could unlock the power, and would be seeking to capture someone to do it for him. His ultimate mission would be to destroy time itself, taking us all down with him. And all because he had received no appreciation for doing his job for all those countless and lonely days, he sought out revenge.

At times, he had been seen stealing innocent people off the streets to see if they could unlock the power for him. It made my stomach turn, to think of what the monster did to them before he disposed of them. However, since he was unsuccessful, we understood what we had to do. He had gotten the hourglass back around fifteen years ago, and had been guarding it ever since. I myself had stepped up to fight him before, but only succeeded in angering him.

The professor interrupted my thoughts, as he wagged his head. "It appears that you have a distress signal coming from there."

"We don't know anyone from that region," declared Sarah.

"You should look anyway."

"So should we just waltz in there and ask where the signal is coming from?"

The professor picked up two heavy-duty multi-purpose backpacks. "Yes, go in there and ask," he said over his shoulder. "The plane is in the lower level, ready yourselves and meet me there in one hour."

Chapter 2

The elevator bell chimed, and door quietly slid open to reveal a cavernous, undefined dark space. Under normal circumstances, we would not be allowed into the deepest level in our multi-level base, the transportation room. Our steps echoed in the room, and the only source of light was the dim fluorescent from the elevator. Suddenly, a single light popped on, revealing Alden hunched over a small consol in the middle of the room.

"We're here now!" I yelled.

"I can tell. Just a moment!" Exactly five seconds later, a powerful engine roared in the inky blackness, filling the entire place with the steady hum of its spinning blades. Two shining beams of blue light came closer and closer, and stopped to rest under a spotlight. It was a biplane. The prop on the front had three turquoise blades, and two small rocket engines positioned next to the stabilizers. It was a silvery sheen of navy and on each side of the fuselage in large, bold silver letters: *Starsteel*. The professor smiled and said, "Your power shield and backpacks full of necessities are stored in the cockpit. The coordinates are already programmed in."

"Do I need to say it?"

"What?"

"You're obsessed with blue." I jokingly commented as Sarah and I climbed into the cockpit.

The professor chuckled, and then slammed a button on his console.

A slow grinding resonance vibrated underneath the plane, and a massive platform materialized out of the metal floor. A square shape of natural light appeared directly above us. The platform rocketed upward, and in moments, we were at the surface. The trees, bushes, and grass parted in front of us, exposing a short asphalt runway that angled upwards sharply. The noise significantly increased from the plane, now beginning to roar with the steady drone of the engines. Seconds later, we were thrust forward and into the air.

We passed over many mountains and valleys. Sarah and I gradually turned our attention toward each other as boredom began to overtake us. It seems we could always find something insignificant to disagree about. Four thousand feet in the air, we began arguing over which button would fire the wing-mounted power lasers. We were on the verge of flipping every switch in the cockpit to find out who was right.

"It's this one."

"No, this one!"

"That one flares the shields!"

"No." I cautioned.

Sarah pressed a button and a high-pitched shriek of pulsing energy surrounded us. Suddenly, a small red object hurled toward us. Luckily, the shield button she had pressed deflected the missile outside of it, throwing us back our seats.

"Uh-oh," she yelped. Immediately she pulled a few levers and flipped some switches. "Using that shield drained a lot of power. We barely have enough energy to keep us in flight. I am rerouting a bit of power now."

The left engine sputtered, howled, and stalled. "Buckle up, and get ready to go down!" Then the right engine struggled to pick up the slack of the failure, but quickly overloaded and blew out from the power surge. The prop was our last hope, but unfortunately, it stalled out. Without warning, the plane nosed and went into a dive. I braced for impact the best I could hoping that the professors handiwork would be enough to protect us.

"In retrospect, I probably should have done something different."

"Yep," I responded rhetorically.

We were on the ground, but the plane had taken quite a bit of damage from the crash. The prop was missing along with several pieces of the wings and body, and both engines were burned out, probably damaged beyond repair. Thanks to the Professor's ingenuity, the cockpit remained intact.

Sarah shook her head muttering things that I was guessing were not very complimentary to monsters.

We had landed in the midst of a forested area, but extremely close to the edge of a cliff overlooking small lake. Off in the distance, we could see the ruins we were heading for positioned on a hill overlooking the lake. The old stone pillars and arches were nothing special, and the grass around them was trampled, indicating someone or something had recently been through there.

At the edge of the forest, we noted the still smoldering patches of grass. "Looks like these monsters are getting smarter. Left before we crashed." Sarah pointed out.

Suddenly we were startled back to reality when we heard the shrill chimes of a ringtone. I edged toward the cockpit, peeked in, and a tiny screen flickered to life, displaying the grainy image of Professor Alden.

"Are you alright?"

"How did you know we crashed?"

"I couldn't be too careful. I installed a tracking device on the plane."

"Well, professor, we kinda have a problem with transportation, if you haven't noticed."

"It's understood. I'll try to find a way to help."

Sparks crackled from under the screen then it abruptly winked off, leaving us alone yet again in the woods. We both trotted off in the direction of the stone ruins, looking for anything that might help us. I skidded to a stop when I heard a voice . . . that sounded like talking Cobra mixed with a British accent.

"Hello Nick. Ssso nice to sssee you again."

Chapter 3

Out of pure instinct, I jumped, drew my blade, and slashed frantically the large green thing behind me. However, even with my speed he easily dodged the deadly arc. As his tail flashed towards me, I thought. *What I did just now was either brave, or completely dumb.*

I knew from the drawings Professor Alden had showed me, I was standing face to face with Wryghten. But I did not recall his presence to be so ominous. I hoped that my years of training and modern fighting skills would give me an advantage over his ancient style of fighting. His power and size were in his favor, while my speed and agility made me a difficult target to hit.

He looks like a normal emerald colored garden snake. However, he is about twenty times that size, over thirty feet long. He also has two small, bony arms that protrude out from the sides of his body, complete with razor sharp claws that look like ivory. Several long lines traced down his sides, and shines a brilliant glow of cobalt. A small circle is on his forehead, and it radiates brightly whenever he uses powers. Dragon teeth and horns complete the horror show, and intelligent reptilian eyes twinkle with savage light.

With over five hundred years of training and experience under his scaly belt, he is more than a match for even the most skilled fighter or swordsman. He would be a formidable foe for a well-equipped army.

The force of his tail was extremely powerful, and knocked me straight through a stone pillar. Moreover, if not for the shield strapped to my arm, the blow could have broken every bone in my body. Still stunned from the impact though, I gasped for air.

Out of nowhere, a small blue blur ran in front of my disoriented gaze and blew something from its mouth. Immediately, I felt a chill came across me as a massive wall of ice formed, allowing me a few seconds to recover. Wryghten slammed against it, but did not make any visible cracks. With one slash from his razor-sharp claws, it collapsed into a pile of blue shards and he barreled through it.

This time, I was prepared. I quickly vaulted over blocks of broken ruins, and slammed my blade into his reptilian face. I rolled backwards, hiding behind a tree to catch my breath.

He swooped down toward me again as I tried to swipe at him. But he knocked me aside as if I was nothing more than a bit of fluff in a storm. I only slid backwards, but felt instant pain in my shoulder and was unable to move. He roared in victory and slashed at me again.

But this time, Sarah jumped in to my rescue. They came to a complete standoff, locked blade to claw. With a roar, he tried to shove her, but she held her ground.

"Move!" exclaimed Sarah.   "Move, Nick, I got him!"

No, she did not have him, and she knew that. Her hands began to shake uncontrollably. Roaring with intimidation, Wryghten pushed forward again, but this time her stance failed. He batted her away, and she landed somewhere out of my sight. I struggled to get up and run in the direction she landed, but was still too weak. So I braced myself for whatever misery might come next.

He grabbed me with his boney arms and the circle on his forehead began to glow. I attempted to break free, but was still too winded to move. Without warning, he discharged a massive bolt of electricity directly toward me.

Realizing I had drastically underestimated his fighting skill, I began to scream in complete agony as I thrashed around trying to break free. Electrical pulses continued through my body as I began to lose consciousness. The pain was simply too intense.

The glowing ring on his forehead faded and he abruptly ceased his attack. My scrambled thoughts were simply too senseless to even formulate a better plan. "Have fun." Wryghten whispered with evident relish.

He then tossed me headfirst into the lake. Deeply fatigued, beaten, and unable to swim, I began to slowly sink below the surface. The last image I saw before I blacked out was Wryghten floating away with my unconscious sister . . .

Chapter 4

"Pii?" a little voice uttered.

"AGH!" I grunted as I slowly pulled myself onto the bank with water sloshing out of my waterlogged clothes. Without thinking, I put my left arm on the ground trying get up. Immediately I yelled in pain, stars dancing in front of my eyes. Through my fevered mind, I racked my brains to recall first aid procedures that I learned from the professor on how to reset a dislocated joint. I squeezed my eyes shut, grit my teeth and slowly rotated my arm to the right. Tears leaked from the corners of my closed eyes from the pain, but I still pushed. The painful snap that came from my arm, made me sigh with relief as the pain subsided almost instantly.

Finally able to focus on something other than pain, I got a good look at my surroundings. To my surprise, much of the lake was frozen solid. A little blue thing stood by, staring at me inquisitively. I grunted, acknowledging his help, but wondered what he was doing here.

When finally got my first good look at him, I realized he was just a mouse. An overgrown mouse at that, about the size of a miniature dog with back legs obviously made for jumping, but much smaller front paws. His small piercing black eyes were set in his small head right above his triangular nose, with long ears that flicked continually. An almost imperceptible mist came from his mouth. His tail was a black zigzag with an azure crystal nestled on the end of it. It glowed, and occasionally pulsed with blue light, emitting small twinkles of frost drifting in all directions. His fur was completely light blue.

"Can you speak, little guy?"

"Pii."

"Can you say anything else?"

"Pii, Pii." He shook his head.

"So you can understand me?"

"Pii!"

The blue mouse energetically ran around, covering the ground in a fine layer of frost wherever his paws touched. His antics made me smile, but thoughts of the earlier battle flooded my mind like a surging tide. The plane was destroyed, my sister had been kidnapped, and Wryghten had so easily prevailed against me. I began to wonder if I would be able to defeat him without outside help.

As anger began to swell in my thoughts, I reflected on how this mouse-like thing had helped me. I beckoned for him to follow, which he did without question. I had made a new ally.

—(::)—

As I sprinted through the forest alongside the equally fast mouse, I hacked through at the overhanging bushes using my sword with ease. We had been on the trail of the Rashidimis, who had been devoted followers of Wryghten (what we called the

16

black monsters) killing them at every opportunity. Nevito froze many of the monsters by breathing on them, freezing them in solid blocks of ice, then smashing them to pieces with his tail. I had named him Nevito, meaning "snow-mouse" in Latin. I had no idea how I had won his trust, but was extremely grateful for his help, knowing I needed someone to watch my back.

As we continued to run, I saw a piece of the wing from our crashed and screeched to a halt plane. Nevito tripped, banging his head.

"Pii . . ." he groaned.

For a moment, I was torn. I could either run after Wryghten, destroying the surviving monsters (which would be fun and satisfying), or rebuild the plane and attack from the air (which would be smart). I knew without a doubt that battling against the monsters would not be a problem, but fighting took time, and time was definitely not on my side. In a split second my decision was made, I turned and charged back in the direction we had just come from, startling the panting Nevito.

Back at the wreckage of the plane, I was able to contact Professor Alden. I had to reconnect a few wires, but I managed. He grinned as he asked, "How are you, my boy? Was your search fruitful?" In as few words as possible, I explained all that had

17

transpired in past hours. "I need help," I added. "The plane is destroyed, Sarah is kidnapped, and I have no idea what to do." The grave expression on the professor's face said it all.

"So he is waiting for you . . . I figured as much. Look in your pack, there is something that there will help you." The professor finished.

I rummaged through the pack at my side. I found my shield, several energy bars, water . . . my hand touched something solid and frigid. I slowly pulled the thing out, an emerald. The late afternoon sun reflected off the gem with rays of light radiating from within. The area around me illuminated from its brilliance.

As I stared into its core, I noted a faint light emanating from inside. I felt a tingle of energy, that suddenly shocked me, throwing me to the ground as my consciousness faded.

Quite different from the bolt that Wryghten had attacked me with, it was not as harsh lightning, but soft and tingly. However, it left me with a deep, radiating headache that made me feel as if a shard of hot glass was being pushed into my cranium. I faintly heard myself screaming.

Nevito, standing close by watched intently.

As I slumped to the ground, the last thought I had before I blacked out was. *NOT AGAIN!*

Chapter 5

"Fii!" a little voice uttered.

"Ughhh . . ." I grunted back.

Stars danced before my eyes as I awoke. I forced my eyes open and reached out to the bright red bush that was in front of me to steady myself, while trying to get to my feet.

"What?" I exclaimed.

When I touched the "bush", I felt a burning sensation and immediately drew my hand back. I realized it was not a bush at all. It let out a short high-pitched growl and backed away several feet. Fascinated, I took a closer and studied it.

The thing looked a lot like Nevito, but its fur was a deep orange-red color, and his stomach had a tan color. On the end of his straw-thin zigzag tail, a small red crystal emitted a constant flame. His paws were also small, but stockier than the slender Nevito. He was crossing his paws in a manner similar to how a person would cross their arms.

"Hello."

"Fii!" he said, and turned his head away indignantly.

My lips cracked as I smiled and thought *how many friends does Nevito have*. Thinking about him, I looked around and saw him sitting on a rock, watching me with a little smile on his mousey face.

As I slowly got to my feet and steadied myself, I found a pulsing blue-colored bubble surrounded me.

What in the world? I thought. Wherever my feet touched the ground, small wisps of smoke drifted off the burned ground. Puzzled at my transformation, and remembering the crystal, I returned to the wreckage.

Back in the cockpit, the screen flickered on and a burst of static filled the air. I waited for a few moments and the image of the professor slowly faded in.

"You blacked out before I had a chance to tell you. Great job. Activating the ships main console so I could track the signal? Ingenious. Couldn't have done better myself."

"Stop mocking me."

"I am deeply sorry, it won't happen again . . ."

"Humph."

"Humph yourself, grouchy." He grinned, and it struck me that he was trying to make me feel better.

Honestly, it has to be the worst day ever to be comforted by Alden, a person who can be gruff and sometimes a bit harsh. Being out in the middle of the woods with a wrecked plane, two oversized mice, and several hundred Rashmidis roaming around would be more than enough to make anybody edgy. I felt like breaking down as well, but had managed to keep my composure so far.

"So," I began. "What does this aura thing do?"

"Aura?" I nodded and moved back to show him the pulsing-blue glow that encased me. Alden suddenly became highly interested. He began taking notes, pictures and even asking questions like, "How do you feel?" and "How is your vision?"

I interrupted his rapid-fire questions with one of my own. "This isn't supposed to happen?"

He dropped his pen and peered up over his round rimmed spectacles. "No, I'm afraid not. That emerald was designed to retain information and images from past events. You know about the hourglass's legend, right?"

I nodded an affirmative.

"This may be a bit of a shock, but . . . the guardian who failed was your father."

Startled by the revelation, the only response I could offer was to stare back at him. I tried to speak, but I could not form a coherent thought. My father was the last guardian, the same one who failed to protect the hourglass. Doubt and suspicion bubbled up and I weakly stated, "But . . . that was over millennia ago. How could I be his son?"

That's what you think? A voice faded into my thoughts.

"Yeah," I responded.

The professor's brow furrowed. "Yeah what?"

"You just asked me what I thought."

"I asked no such thing."

Suddenly, the look of confusion vanished from Alden's face. In place of it, a mixture of emotions came forth anger, resentment, and even a bit of fear. He straightened in his seat, and abruptly shut off the screen without speaking another word.

Chapter 6

Staring at the now blank screen, I wondered how I should react to a near-imaginary voice that had just intruded into my mind, much like a mouse. A mouse scratches, chews, and nibbles its way into your house. Very much uninvited, worming his way deep in there, but you have no way of getting him out without completely burning it down in frustration.

Always the joker, aren't you?

"Well, of course. Expect any less?" I realized I was speaking out loud. I berated myself, and then remembered we were in the middle of nowhere; it didn't matter.

I am assuming that you would not believe a little voice in your head.

"You better believe it." I replied, hoping I was not going crazy.

"Then how is this, is this better?"

"Yeah . . . wait, what?"

I whirled around to the direction the voice came from, and I nearly jumped out of my blue sneakers. With sandy blond hair, blue eyes, and a wide grin, he looked eerily like me. Dressed in a blue robe, he looked like a monk. However, a brilliant cerulean and gold broadsword hanging at his side eliminated any thought of him being peaceful person.

"Hello, Nick."

"You aren't real, are you?"

"No.   And in fact, only you can see me. Essentially, it is your imagination that has brought me forth."

"Okay . . . so, um, what's with the getup? Are you supposed to be a nun or something?"

"As I said, a joker. No, I am a guardian. And your father."

"Yeah," I replied. "I can't get over that part."

I gestured to the plane. "What am I thinking of now?"

"You want to fix it. Let's get to work, shall we?"

Hours passed and the plane gradually came together with the help of Feuto (Latin for Fire-Mouse), taking care of the welding. Hoping for the best, with a groan and a shudder, the engines started up. Quietly and without speaking the image of my father faded away as Feuto and Nevito scurried into the cockpit. Feeling proud of all we had accomplished, I hauled myself in as well.

With a push of a button, the engines revved up with a high-pitched whine. I tilted the flaps down, thrusting us upward. With push of another button, we blasted off into the twilight.

Chapter 7

As the plane sailed on, I climbed up to a standing position on top of the upper wing set, mounted just above the cockpit. It was an extremely crazy stunt, considering that any powerful gust of wind could send me hurling towards the ground.

I looked down and to my surprise, saw the image of my father sitting in the cockpit. He motioned to me, trying to say something. I crouched down in an attempt to catch what he was saying, but the wind snatched his words away. I tapped my ear in response. He made a twirling motion, and then pointed towards the ground.

Below I saw a strange mix of what appeared to be movie equipment, bulldozers, cranes and large thermal, orange neon tents. We had located the encampment of the Rashmidis.

My dad gave me thumbs up, then rolled the plane to the left. I jumped off and drew my sword, aiming for the lake that was right next to their camp. I hit the water, but used my speed powers to minimize the impact. After surfacing, I swam as fast as I could to the shore. To my surprise, I recognized that the monsters did not even see my dive or the plane that was flying around.

I then noticed that two more specks were falling from the craft; Feuto and Nevito. They both landed squarely on a monster's angled face, who in turn smacked himself on his own head to get them off.

His overzealous effort to get rid of the two mice was a bit too powerful and he exploded into green goo. Only then did the rest of the monsters take notice.

Upon realizing our presence, they quickly engaged us in a full-blown battle. The mice were actually very accomplished fighters, as there were plenty of monsters who burned in an inferno or were frozen into big blocks of ice, only to be shattered.

After several minutes of fighting I was drenched in sweat, my arms were laden, and my hands felt like they were glued to the sword. The only reason I had survived was that they attacked one at a time.

I slipped on a patch of wet grass, and as I went down, the monster I was fighting bellowed in victory, raising his black and green fist. He suddenly screamed and burst into goo. In his place stood Sarah. One of the mice had apparently set her free. She grinned and ran between monsters swinging her sword in every direction possible. Chaos and confusion disoriented the mass of monsters as they tried to assess this new threat.

Her distraction allowed me to regain my strength. I began to attack them again, and within seconds, the battle was over. Just as I was about to run to Sarah to celebrate our victory, I heard the voice I never wanted to hear again. "Hello, young hero. Greetingsss!"

We all yelped and jumped up, as I whirled around to confront him. But he opened his mouth and spewed a fireball the size of a basketball at me. It hit me square in the chest. Just as suddenly as he appeared, Wryghten floated up and slithered off between the trees.

Within seconds, it exploded.

Chapter 8

I coughed.

Painful flashes of light danced around inside my skull, reminding me of the damage inflicted. Finally daring to open my eyes, I found myself lying on a sandy riverbank.

I looked down at my torn shirt exposing my burned stomach. It looked bad, but I knew it could have been much worse had I not fallen in the water to douse it. Looking at the sun, I estimated I had been out for more than an hour. I struggled to get up, but a sudden burst of pain left me clutching my stomach and gasping for air.

Suddenly, Nevito and Feuto burst out of the bushes, followed by my sister.

"You're so dumb!" Sarah yelled, which is how I knew that she was relieved to see me. Feuto and Nevito made happy noises (I had no idea what they were saying).

"Hey," I breathlessly uttered.

"Hey? Is that all? You just got blown sky-high!"

"I can see why you're so upset . . ."

"Upset? I am well past that! I was afraid that. . ." Her voice trailed off.

I understood. I had felt the same kind of fear when Wryghten had taken her. And her admitting fear to me, the one she was closest to, was rare.

I stared at the sky, trying to see if there were any signs of Wryghten flying around. Sarah suddenly started running toward the forest, as did Feuto and Nevito. I ran after them.

Several monsters were in close pursuit as we ran past the plane. I felt a growing resentment knowing these attacks had just been relentless and that we had been at the mercy of these monsters, I was weary of it.

The world warped around me, as I turned and charged at them. My thoughts seemed to become dazed, I continued to strike like a maniac, and my mind seemed to go into an automatic program mode: slash, stab, block and roll. Time seemed to elongate, making me feel like I had been fighting for hours, when in reality it had only been for mere minutes. I continued to swing until nothing remained. I looked around me to see that everything had been destroyed, and had even sliced off one of the plane wings. Everyone gaped at me.

A horrible realization frightened me: Wryghten was right. I could be his servant and take over the world; he saw how much potential I had. I scowled, walked over to the plane and began to repair the broken wing.

Reflecting on all that had just occurred; I was certain now – we must kill him.

Chapter 9

"Our hastily assembled airplane seems to be holding together well!"

"Pii!"

"Fii!"

I grinned, and opened up the throttle a little more. We screamed forward, and I checked on my sleeping sister. Fueto looked determined, crossing his arms. Nevito looked queasy, holding his hands (excuse me, paws) to his tiny mouth. They all looked tired but willing to fight.

Hearing an explosion on the left, I looked to see an enormous fireball heading our way. I yelled out and rolled to the right, the missile scraping us by inches. Awakened by the explosion, Sarah quickly assessed the entire situation, and yelled, "We have no weapons, and we have to make a run for it!" I nodded in agreement.

I pushed the throttle as far as it could go, and continued. Then saw it. A massive floating caldera with boiling magma, no place to land and a giant floating lizard (Wrygthen) shooting fireballs at us.

"How did he make something like that?" I yelled as I rolled to avoid another fireball.

"Let me see!" Sarah leaned out, and quickly studied the island. She leaned back into her seat and yelled, "It looks like he used the power of the hourglass to gather the rocks and pockets of magma to make this!"

Shocked, I yelled back, "I thought the legend said that the power can only be unlocked by people pure of heart!"

"I thought so too!" she answered.

I knew that eventually, the plane would lose its energy, or Wryghten would make a lucky hit. Taking a chance, I rolled over towards him and tried to charge at him.

It did not work out quite as planned.

He raised his claw in the air, and suddenly a pulsing, purple shield enveloped the island. With us going so fast, we were unable to stop in time, and dove through the colorful lights.

At first, nothing happened.

All of a sudden, the plane started to fall apart as if it was held together with glue. There was little I could do except guide the remaining parts to the caldera. "Brace yourselves!" was the only thing I could say before we crashed into the side of the mountain.

Chapter 10

I struggled to my feet, trying to shuffle backwards and block while balancing on one foot at lip of the caldera. Wryghten laughed with evident maniacal joy at what terror he had caused.

"Come down, young heroesss!" His amplified voice rang across the magma. "Come down and meet your 'maker', as you call it!" He raised his arms yet again, and we ducked in anticipation. Massive red-hot stones began to boil up in the middle, cooling off and bonding together forming a rocky island over fifty feet in diameter, with several smaller ones leading to it, like stepping-stones.

Staring at me with piercing eyes, he motioned with his hands for me to come closer. Seeing no other options, I called for Sarah and the mice to follow me as we began hopping from stone to stone. Nevito was the last to jump onto the island and when his paws touched it, the stepping-stones we had just come across collapsed into the magma.

Wryghten's toothy approximation of a smile, complete with his bold statement disturbed us all. "You ssshall not leave thisss placcce alive."

We stared each other down for several minutes, waiting to see who would make the first move. He finally got impatient. "Sssince you will not back down, I will ssshow you something, yesss I will." He motioned upward. Remaining keenly alert, we looked, thinking it might be a trick. Above, in a bluish nimbus of energy, the hourglass floated at the very top of his purple energy field.

Sarah gasped and exclaimed, "The hourglass!"

"Behold." Wryghten confidently stated.

With a cold feeling in the pit of my stomach, I began to piece together his plan: his well-thought out, massive, dangerous plan.

Wryghten turned to me as if he sensed my thoughts. "You underssstand now."

"You wouldn't."

"Ahh, but I would, young hero."

"Why? Why destroy everything?"

"Thisss world . . . it hasss too many." He smiled again, as if it would make it all better.

"That makes no sense." I scowled.

"Too many benefitsss. Too many luxuriesss. Too many living!"

"Do you really want the entire world to suffer? Because you were wronged once?"

He snarled, as if my words burned him. "NO. I was wronged every day, ever since I was born, for a thousand years. And for that, the world will suffer."

Suddenly, the world outside the force field began to change. "Umm, Nick? Something is happening," called Sarah.

I looked around in horror, "You don't say?"

"Ha! Petty mortal." He grinned even wider, if it was even possible. "Once I am finissshed with you, I will dessstroy time using the hourglass. I will create dimensionsss whenever I pleassse, and destroy them when they become a bore! Mark thisss in your insssignificant mindsss. You are the lassst living beingsss!"

After his last words, the world that previously surrounded us, disappeared into darkness, as if someone had covered us in black wool. The only light that remained was from the hourglass, the force field, and the magma.

Without thinking, and without a plan, I charged toward the green scaly beast.

Chapter 11

Repeatedly, I slashed at Wryghten trying to do some sort of damage, hoping that one of my blows would penetrate his armor and wound him. While fighting, I was vaguely aware of Sarah, Feuto and Nevito attacking the monsters he had summoned during my first charge. I edged around the scaly beast in front of me, trying to determine the weakest point to attack him. Nevertheless, he managed to defend against all my efforts with relative ease as if he were a hundred swordsmen instead of an awkwardly large, green, floating reptile.

"Yesss," he hissed. "You are quite entertaining. But it isss due time for you to perisssh!" Unleashing a massive bolt of lightning that streaked in all directions, momentarily paralyzing the others, but . . . I thrust my sword into the rock beneath me, grounding myself against the charge. With a yell, I sprinted forward, scoring multiple hits on his tail and body. I jabbed my blade into the earth and swung around using my momentum to propel me around. I charged again, and on this pass, I cut off a larger bit of his tail.

His roar of pain made it all worth it. His body crackled with random bolts of energy, frying the air with its power. His words made no sense but I did not need to hear them in order to understand his rage, pain and absolute disbelief at the severity of his wounds.

A sudden gust of wind threatened to tear us off the giant floating island. Still trapped in the blue sphere, the hourglass appeared to be supporting the island of rock, and creating the field that was stopping time from reversing. It was becoming apparent we were not going to be able to defeat Wyrghten by ourselves. He would tear us apart with little effort, and we could not hold him off alone for long.

As if she knew what I was thinking, Sarah ran around with Feuto, clashing with random monsters that managed to survive our previous pass. I chuckled darkly, beckoning Nevito to follow. "Piiiii!" he said, nodding as if he understood a determined look on his face. We both charged at Wyrghten, who was just regaining strength from the loss of part of his tail, and swung to face us.

Grinning, I jumped and exchanged a flurry of blows so fast that the air hummed around me. He slashed back with his claws, keeping time with my blows.

"I wasss toying with you before, now it isss time to finish thisss." His flat, serious tone penetrated my being, as if he had spoken with vibrations and not words. Sparks flew, setting fires on the ground. The fires proved to be a certain distraction, while still exchanging strikes I absentmindedly stepped into a fire, igniting my pants. I swatted the flames out, but he took advantage of it and struck me hard, throwing me backwards, almost falling off the island. Nevito saw me on the ground and created a shield of ice, buying me enough time to recover and get back to my feet. "Thanks." I mumbled, and promptly ran around the barrier.

The sight I saw next made my heart turn. Sarah and Feuto were encased in a blue bubble, exactly like the one that was holding the Hourglass.

Seeing red, I yelled out a feeble, "Hey!" and without thinking, charged forward.

He easily knocked me aside. "Ssso tired already?" gloating yet again. He floated forward slowly without waiting for an answer, bashing me as he went. I struggled to block his powerful swipes, but took several of them. I fell to one knee, struggling to stand.

With a final snarl, he slammed the full weight of himself on top of me. He picked me up like a rag doll, and knocked my sword away.

I . . . had lost.

"Persssonally, I would have enjoyed you being my willing asisssstant," he said, spitting out the last word, "but clearly that isss not going to happen. How many timesss will I have to break your arm for you to sssee?"

Do not give up, I heard in my sub-consciousness.

"Dad?"

Wyghten looked around inquisitively, saying, "What?"

My final gift is this. My power. My strength. My will. Use it, and do not GIVE UP!

The memory crystal, which I had taken from my pack next to the wreckage of the plane suddenly shattered. Wryghten glanced at it, and I used the opportunity to wriggle out of his grip on jump on top of his head. He yowled in frustration and tried to push me off by flicking his head up. Instead, I used his motion like a springboard and shot straight up, right toward the hourglass. Out of pure frustration, he fired a flame-ball at me. Without hesitation, I threw my sword toward it like a tomahawk. The fire-bomb and blade collided, and the resulting explosion pushed me even higher. Wryghten realized my plan too late, and in vain shot off another dozen fireballs in my direction.

At that exact moment I touched the hourglass and it's power ran through me creating a force field that enveloped me. My body began to glow with a blue aura, growing stronger every second. Energy streamed through my body when I thought I had none. With renewed vigor, I jumped to retrieve my sword and drove it as hard as I could into Wryghten's forehead, pouring energy into the blade metal itself.

It hit home.

His scream was so loud and powerful, stones beneath us began cracking. A beam of red light shone from the stab point, and his whole body began to glow. He began writhing as if there were a million ants crawling on him. At that moment, the energy sphere binding Sara and Feuto collapsed; they scrambled free.   And we all saw what was about to happen.

"Hit the deck!" My sister screamed. We all fell to the ground.

"How isss thisss posssible!"   His last words destroyed much of the rock because of its terrible vibrating power.   The light increased, then Wryghten's body shattered with an explosion . . .

Chapter 12

Smoke eerily wafted up from spot where Wryghten had gone nova.

Sarah coughed.

Nevito and Feuto got to their feet, whimpering a bit, but all right.

"Nick." Sarah coughed again and sat up. "You should fix this." She weakly gestured around her. I crouched by her, helping her get to her feet.

"What do you mean?" I said.

"You need to put time back."

"I have no idea how."

Nevito and Feuto crawled over to us, completely covered in white with dust.

An ominous rumble sounded beneath my feet, and the rocks shivered.

Silence ensued for a few more seconds, then without warning, a mighty groan sounded, and the ground shook with much greater force, nearly throwing us of our feet.

"Um, Nick? Today would be nice!" My sister cried out in alarm.

Globs of magma sputtered from cracks in the rock, and crevasses began to form.

"NICK?" Sarah yelped, now with an edge of panic in her voice. If I was not so tired and focused on not losing my balance I would have responded.

The island was beginning to show massive cracks running throughout. The groaning began to sound all around us, and the indigo shield that had been around the island was clearly beginning to waver. The mice were jumping from rock to rock, clearly having a tough time staying out of the hungry grasp of the boiling molten soup.

At this point, I was in no position to yell back as I was struggling to maintain my balance, and not fall into the magma myself.

Suddenly, the hourglass flew out of my hand, and began to glow again. But this time, instead of a blue light, it was pure white. It enveloped everything including the mice. The soft, persistent glow pulsed once then I knew no more.

I was in mid-strike with my blade, swinging it in a deadly ark . . . towards Sarah. She blocked, but then looked confused herself. We quickly dropped our swords and began to search around us. We found ourselves on top of the grassy hill that we had been sparring on two days ago. Nevito and Feuto were also next to us, looking confused and dazed.

I found the hourglass in my hand, still glowing. I suddenly realized the hourglass had rebooted time to two days earlier, almost as if nothing had happened.

"Sarah?"

"Yeah?" She looked at me expectantly.

"You remember everything that happened, right?"

"Yes . . . Huh." She glanced at her watch. "It's two days ago! I mean, it's two days ago today."

"So, we brought time back? But how? I don't even know how that happened!" Sarah shook her head, completely mystified over the entire situation.

Soft steps behind us made me jump to my feet, as adrenaline from the fight was still pouring through my veins. I whirled around to confront the face of Professor Alden.

"I was wondering where you were." His graying mustache quivered as he spoke, and he scowled at us.

"You have a distress signal coming a couple hundred miles from where we are in Canada. Come inside for a briefing!" He stalked off, leaving us more confused than before.

"How come he doesn't remember anything, but we do?" My sister contemplated aloud.

And I have a question. "Why did you yell out 'Dad' when Wryghten was holding you?"

"I didn't tell you? I thought I did."

"No, you didn't."

I quickly explained all that had transpired when she was a hostage, including the help from Nevito and Feuto, and gaining my father's memory crystal.

When I finished, Sarah questioned. "So he gave you powers?"

"Yes," I thought again and said, "Actually, I'm not sure. He gave me a "gift", but I'm not even sure what it does."

41

I was about to say more, but the professor suddenly charged back over the hill. Out of breath, he yelled, "What are you holding?"

"Well, it's the hourglass."

"How did you . . ."

"Get it?" In as few words as possible, I explained our travels and battle with Wryghten.

The professor nodded, acting as if I had just told him that I had taken a leisurely trip to the grocery store.

"Well, it makes sense. And I have absolutely no memory of it."

"Also, the distress signal. It's fake." I suggested.

"Oh, that? No, it is very real. It is from another group."

"Another group?"

"I suppose it is time to tell you. Come Inside."

After we had taken had showers, eaten, and settled into our seats we began telling all that had happened. I mainly spoke and Sarah filled in what I forgotten. Professor Alden sat with a thoughtful look on his face when we had finished. After several minutes of silence, the professor finally spoke, clearing his throat and declared, "Time Squeeze."

"I'm sorry?" I inquired, not understanding that term.

"Time Squeeze. You have activated an extremely unpleasant and dangerous process known as Time Squeeze."

Sarah shook her head and said, "You're going to have to walk us through what that is, doc."

"Try and follow this. Basically, you killed Wryghten, correct?"

We both nodded.

"Well, you killed him two days in the future, but then you traveled two days in the past, when he wasn't dead yet. However, he really did die, so the two outcomes can't be possible."

I shook my head, I did not get it. "Where are you going with this?"

"You didn't really go back in time. You simply copied time, and then pasted it three days into the future, which is today. Wryghten was dead yesterday, but he is alive today."

To which my sister replied, "I still don't see how this is bad."

"Don't you see?" The professor exploded. "The rules of the entire known universe have effectively been shredded!"

For several minutes, we all sat mute as rocks.

Sarah was the first to break the silence. "What will happen?"

The professor paled as he answered. "Imagine this, a world where there are no physical rules, no possibilities, yet endless possibilities. Gravity would become just an idea, no longer a reality. Time would be the same forever, and we would slowly descend into madness and oblivion as time begins to slowly tear itself apart. Is that a good enough picture for you?"

My sister almost opened her mouth, as if to say something, but shut it quickly.

I spoke up again and asked, "So how can we stop it? And how long will it take the 'process' to fully take affect?"

The professor scratched his head, and then said, "I will answer the second question first, as it is easier to answer. It will take around four years for the full extent of the time rip to become obvious. The first question is a bit more difficult. What we could do is . . ."

I interrupted. "Couldn't we just break the hourglass?"

"Heavens no! Don't you understand? The hourglass is the representation of time. In other words, the hourglass is time. Also, it would take a great deal of energy to make a single crack. We considered it a while ago, but . . ."

Again, I interrupted. "We, who are we?"

"'We' are five caretakers, or professors, whatever you want to call us. We each have two kids that we are responsible to protect, train and guide. Our responsibility is tremendous; you ten are the last remnants of the Lost Kingdom that I have taught you about."

We both nodded, knowing we had received extensive lessons on the mysterious kingdom that did not have a place in the history books, but had really written it themselves. They were not mentioned anywhere in any ancient writings, and had mysteriously disappeared when the hourglass was last stolen, over seven hundred years ago.

"So what happens now?" Asked Sarah.

Everybody, including the mice, stared at Alden expectantly.

He took off his glasses and while cleaning them, spoke in a low voice.

"In order for us to reverse Time Squeeze, we must discover if in any of the Lost Kingdom writings there are solutions to our predicament. Otherwise, we may never have a chance in reversing the phenomenon."

He stood up and positioned the glasses back on his head.

"Since you destroyed the Starsteel, I will design and build a sturdier and faster version of it." He leaned toward us both and whispered, "I have a feeling that you're going to do a lot of traveling."

I grinned and retorted, "Well, what are we waiting for?"

End of Book 1.

Matthew David

At the age of seven, Matthew's imagination became very evident when he created his own comic strip including custom characters, consistent artwork and original story lines. Now after two years of development his first book - Time Squeeze has come to fruition. Writing is a passion and he one day hopes to pursue a career in one of the many paths of creative journalism. He is an accomplished competitive bowler, is homeschooled and enjoys reading and family time, along with his dog in Sacramento, California.

Made in the USA
Charleston, SC
10 December 2012